SHREE HANUMAN CHALISA

SHREE HANUMAN CHALISA

TRANSLATED AND COMMENTED BY

BHASKAR SHARAD

RUPA

Dedicated to

Neem Karoli Baba

Published by
Rupa Publications India Pvt. Ltd 2026
161-B/4, Gulmohar House,
Yusuf Sarai Community Centre,
New Delhi 110049

Sales centres:
Bengaluru Chennai
Hyderabad Kolkata Mumbai

P-ISBN: 978-93-5352-660-3
E-ISBN: 978-93-5352-009-0

First impression 2026

10 9 8 7 6 5 4 3 2 1

Printed in India

श्रीगुरु चरन सरोज रज निजमनु मुकुरु सुधारि ।
बरनउँ रघुबर बिमल जसु जो दायकु फल चारि ।।

I take dust from the lotus feet of the Guru,
And cleanse my mirror akin heart. Then
I speak and spread the impeccable glory of 'Ram'
Who is the giver of the four fruits of life.

"गुरुकृपा हि केवलं"—Only by the grace of Guru, one is delivered. But Who is a Guru? A true Guru is a SEER (Drsta), the one who has seen the eternal truth. When a Guru arrives in one's life, slowly all his impressions (good or bad) are wiped out and One began to behold the truth as it is. In other words, he becomes a child. When a seeker, with faith in the wisdom and understanding of his Guru, approaches him with reverence (taking dust from his feet), Guru cleanses the soul of his pupil from modifications of Mind.

With such state of mind, Shri Tulasi Das states:

**I believe that Shri Tulasi Das wrote Hanuman Chalisa just before starting his Ramcharitmanas. The reason behind it is this line "बरनउँ रघुबर बिमल जसु" The story of impeccable glory of Shri Ram is Ramayana. So before starting his grand epic, Shri Tulasi Das is invoking the blessing of Lord Hanuman.*

When anyone starts the journey of education in any subject, he starts with accepting few facts of which he does not know the reason. As he grows in his studies he understands the basics behind those rote facts. One such fact is that the speaking and spreading the name and glory of "Ram" brings him before the truth. Many seekers have been delivered through this path. However, scientific reason is yet to be explained. Gurus stress on direct experience of effectiveness of this path, not bothering to explain the reason behind it. The path of a seeker starts with faith, not blind faith, or acceptance of everything presented before him but a trust in the guidance of Guru. That all his questions will be answered to his satisfaction along the way.

**Readers who do not know about Shri Ram are advised to read Ramayana.*

Speaking and spreading glory of Lord Ram brings to seeker four fruits of Life i.e Artha, Dharm, Kama and Moksha. This simply means that he attains everything attainable in this life and after life. Shri Ram is the King of this creation and his grace provides one everything.

बुद्धिहीन तनु जानिके, सुमिरौं पवन-कुमार ।
बल बुधि विद्या देहु मोहिं, हरहु कलेस बिकार ।।

O, Lord Hanuman! I am devoid of wisdom.
Still listen to my song.
Bestow on me–Strength, Intelligence, and Knowledge,
And peel off my mental and physical afflictions.

Devoid of wisdom does not mean without knowledge. It means devoid of pre conceived notions, devoid of biases and devoid of ego. In the spiritual path, only enemy is ego. Kabir wrote that "The path of love is very narrow in which two cannot be accommodated." As a seeker moves forward in this path, his ego vanishes or expands so much to including everyone in it (both are one and same). It is like saying as one renounces his desires, nature is at his disposal. When one surrenders completely, he has all the powers in the world. Scientifically, as light is wave and particle at the same time.

With reverence and faith when one bows before Lord Hanuman, he bestows strength, intelligence, and Knowledge to him, if this is not enough, he also removes the mental afflictions so that one does not deviates from the right path. One point to be noted here is that if the mind is not at peace; power, money and knowledge is useless. Ravana had all of them but we remember him as a villain.

जय हनुमान ज्ञान गुन सागर ।
जय कपीस तिहुं लोक उजागर ।।

O Hanuman! You are an ocean of wisdom and morals.
O Chief among monkeys! The three worlds
are resplendent by thee. (1)

Who is Hanuman? Next few lines give us a glimpse of Hanuman. Glimpse because Hanuman is so immense that describing him in few lines is not possible. These lines are indicative in nature not exhaustive. Shri Tulasi Das starts with the qualities of Hanuman.

Hanuman is Ocean of wisdom and morals. He knows everything and whatever he does, he follows the morals. One good example is from Valmiki Ramayana. When Hanuman was searching Sita in the Palace of Ravana at Lanka in night, he also checked its inner quarters where wives and other female companions of Ravana were sleeping, many in compromising positions. In this situation, a doubt arose in the mind of Hanuman on the correctness of his conduct. He contemplated the situation and concluded that as a spy his duty is to search Sita and in this endeavor his conduct is proper. Similar concept comes in Bhagwat Gita

when Shri Krishna talks about "Swadharma." Morality is very subjective and it depends upon time, place, and culture. Nature is designed such that conflicts are bound to appear. Hanuman is always following morals even when it does not suit one's temperament.

The three Worlds are resplendent with Hanuman. Many sentences in spiritual path are very literal but one may not comprehend it properly due to limited exposure. This may be an allusion to the white light which higher yogis experience during meditation and attributing it to Hanuman. However, for our understanding, we may consider it to describe the fame of Hanuman. The fame of Hanuman is equal in Heaven, Earth, and Hell. In Ramayana, there are numerous instances where Hanuman solved the problem when everyone failed. He was the last resort. Everybody knew this hence his fame was unparalleled.

रामदूत अतुलित बल धामा ।
अंजनि-पुत्र पवनसुत नामा ॥

You are a reliable messenger of 'Ram',
And You have immense strength.
You are known as the Son of 'Anjani'
And called a 'boy of Wind'. (2)

What is the relation between Shri Ram and Shri Hanuman? It is very difficult to realize Shri Ram because he is so pious. His purity makes him difficult to be attained by mere mortals. This may lead to disillusionment among his devotees. So, he has his messenger: Hanuman. Hanuman is the easiest deity to be realized. Hanuman leads devotees to Shri Ram. As soon as a person takes one step towards Shri Ram, Shri Ram sends Hanuman to him as guiding light. Through continuous purification by Hanuman, a devotee is made fit to achieve Shri Ram. Hanuman has immense strength. This gives a devotee an idea about Shri Ram. If his messenger is so powerful, how powerful Raghav is.

In the legend about Hanuman, he was born of 'Anjana' and 'Kesari', a monkey princess and prince respectively. He was born by the blessing of wind god "Vayu." Hence Hanuman is also

called "Son of Anjana" and "Boy of Wind." There are some experts who claim that Hanuman was human of monkey tribe (Kind of a Tribe living in jungles). However, this claim has no base according to Valmiki Ramayan. This can be ascertained from two incidents of Valmiki Ramayan:

1. When Bali (A monkey king) accused Shri Ram of treachery for killing him from behind the bush, Shri Ram gave many reasons. One of the reasons was: Since in hunting killing a beast from behind is not wrong, so piercing Bali from behind was correct as he was but a monkey. As Hanuman and Bali were of same species, Hanuman was a Monkey.

2. When Hanuman was caught by the Ravana's soldiers and his tail was put on fire, by the grace of Sita Hanuman was not burned. This

led Hanuman to ponder: How is that this fire does not burn me and I feel no pain? If the tail of Hanuman was not real, why such thought will ever occur in his mind. Hence, Hanuman was a monkey.

However, Hanuman had the power to assume any shape, so it is of no great significance whether he was a monkey or a human. But I took great pain to explain this point because I find it very amusing and offending that Humans are ready to accept Shri Ram to be born as a Homo Sapiens but they doubt Hanuman to be born as a monkey. I see it as a hubris of humankind.

महावीर विक्रम बजरंगी ।
कुमति निवार सुमति के संगी ॥

You are a great hero, have extreme courage,
and have an exceptionally strong body.
You are the destroyer of illusion,
And you are a friend of pure and pious. (3)

Hanuman was a hero. Hanuman is a hero and he will remain a hero in future. He has exceptionally strong body and he is courageous. A seeker under the refuge of Hanuman knows that he brings out the hero in them. As a result, a devotee of hanuman fears nothing because he knows that he has been taken care of. The path to Shri Ram is treacherous and full of pit falls. Only a devotee as good as hanuman could reach Shri Ram. As a result, by the time a seeker reaches Shri Ram, he becomes Hanuman, a hero personified. When "Indrajit" virtually killed Shri Ram and Shri Lakhsman in Lanka war, Hanuman did not lose courage and brought medicines which cure them. Only a devotee like Hanuman could protect his adorable god. Such instances are rare if not the only one.

Hanuman is destroyer of Illusion. He can pierce the veil of Maya. In Valmiki Ramayan, Sugreev the

monkey king sent his troops in four directions to search for Sita giving them one month time for the same. The army under the leadership of 'Angada' the monkey prince was sent to south which included Hanuman and Jambavan. One month passed but the group could not locate Sita. They camped at the shore of the Ocean contemplating revolt and suicide. However, Hanuman through his reasoning power brought the group back to senses. When Sugreev first saw Shri Ram, he was afraid of him considering Shri Ram to be an assassin sent by Bali. But Hanuman counselled Sugreev and rest is history.

Hanuman is a friend of pure and pious. As per Ramcharitmanas, Hanuman brought Bibhisan, the brother of Ravana under the fold of Shri Ram. Meeting of Tulasi Das with Hanuman is a famous folklore. Even today, guidance of Hanuman is felt by millions of people. Every day cities of India

wake up to songs of Hanuman Chalisa. Hanuman can be felt by each heart when it is pure. That emotion can only be experienced not explained. If you want to feel Hanuman, serve someone with clear heart. He will come verily.

कंचन बरन बिराज सुबेसा ।
कानन कुण्डल कुंचित केसा ।।

Your complexion is golden and you
are elegantly dressed,
You have sported earrings,
And have curly hair. (4)

Once the qualities of Hanuman are known to readers, Mind at once wanders to the physical aspects of him. How does he look? What does he wear?

Shri Tulasi Das answers:

Hanuman is of golden complexion. Gold has a high place in Indian mindset. Anything golden signifies richness, something of high value. This means that the Hanuman's look gives an impression of aristocracy. Also, most prevalent Monkeys of India are of golden hue. Color of Wheat is very much Golden. Many people of India are wheatish. If we take all the above in account, Hanuman face was wheatish to look at but due to his high spiritual effulgence, he gave an aura of gold. His face shined with splendor. Hanuman has curly hair and hc is elegantly dressed with earrings in his earlobes. It is said that Shri Tulasi

Das had met Hanuman, so he is very literal in his description.

A seeker may learn from this description that outer appearance is as important for sadhana as the inner world. Hanuman is said to be in continuous sadhana since he is chanting "Ram Ram" repeatedly. Still, he maintains personal hygiene and manages good look. A seeker must maintain a happy disposition so that the heart of persons who come to them is filled with happiness. It is a very difficult ask for a Sadhak but it is required. If one chants the name of Ram, such mental state gradually dawns to him.

हाथ बज्र औ ध्वजा बिराजै ।
काँधे मूँज जनेऊ साजै ॥

You hold a thunderbolt and a flag in your hand.
You have a sacred thread of grass over your shoulders. (5)

This description of Hanuman describes a major aspect of the Sanatan Dharma. In Sanatan Dharma, Rituals and Violence are accepted.

Rituals play a very important part in the life of any being. They give a sense of stability in flux of nature. As the wheel of time churns, these rituals give a sense of continuity. Without rituals, everything is so ephemeral. Take an example of Marriage ceremony. As two persons wed, people who assemble talk about their marriages or other rituals, what incidents happened then, how that ceremony was arranged etc. In such discussions, they remember their elders and their long traditions. Most of the rituals of India have Vedic history. As one look at his own sacred thread and the sacred thread wore by Hanuman, one feels connected to him. Hanuman is not outside us. He is one among us.

Violence is a reality of Nature. It was there and it will be there. Our Gods have fought wars and killed people. Any religion who does not consider this aspect of nature is incomplete. When Shri Krishna showed his true body to Arjuna, Arjuna was terrified. Because he saw Shri Krishna originating, sustaining, and devouring beings each instant. Every second, beings are created, maintained, and destroyed. Sanatan dharma accepts this ferocious view of Nature and spiritualizes it. A seeker is continuously at war with outer and inner world. Nature and conflict are synonyms; a devotee of Shri Ram and Hanuman knows this.

शंकर सुवन केसरीनंदन ।
तेज प्रताप महा जग वन्दन ।।

O manifested 'Shankar'! O the happiness of 'Kesari'!
Your magnificence is great.
You are praised by the whole universe. (6)

Shankar is Adi Yogi, the one who accepted the poison for the creation. Abode of Shankar is on Mount Kailash. Far away from the world, he is ever steadfast in his yoga. Hanuman is manifested Shankar. He lives among us. Even today, he is living between us. He is guiding seekers towards the right path. He is serving the needy. He is continuously chanting the name of Ram. He is the perfect amalgamation of Gyaan, Karma, and Bhakti Yoga (the three pillars of Yoga). As a result, his magnificence is great and he is praised by everyone.

Becoming Hanuman is very difficult but a seeker can take his example. He may gain some knowledge, serve some persons, and do some worship. If one steadfastly does this, he will gradually advance in his sadhana.

विद्यावान गुणी अति चातुर ।
राम काज करिबे को आतुर ।।

Your knowledge is complete.
You're immensely skilled and clever.
You are eager to perform
the duties of and for 'Ram'. (7)

Knowledge of Shri Ram is complete knowledge. When one understands the alchemy of Shri Ram one knows everything. Who is Shri Ram? How he conducts his affairs? Why he took his birth as human form? These are the questions that baffles the mind of a devotee. Gradually through purgation of soul, an understanding of mystery comes, veil of Maya is removed, and one beholds the truth. One of the easiest and effective method to achieve this is to chant the name of Shri Ram. As a seeker advances towards complete knowledge, he automatically becomes skilled and clever.

Every being, sentient, or non-sentient, is performing duties of and for Ram. What is duty for Ram is best explained from the life of Sampati in Valmiki Ramayan. The story of Sampati is as under:

Sampati and Jatayu, the two brothers were exceedingly powerful and proud vultures. One day they decided to race towards the sun. As they approached the sun, their wings began to burn due to the heat. To save Jatayu, the wings of Sampati was scorched by fire and he fell at the Vindhya mountains. Devoid of power and bereft of strength, in hunger he began to contemplate suicide. However, a Sage Nishakara foretold him that when Shri Ram will take birth on earth, his wife Sita will be abducted by Ravana and you will witness their flight. Then you will have to show the way to despaired monkeys. Sampati trusting the Seer's words, waited for more than a century. When in search of Sita in southern region, the army of Monkeys under the command of Angada at the shore of Ocean were dispirited and without hope, Sampati told them about the whereabouts of Sita, giving life back to Monkeys.

Just to tell the whereabouts of Sita, Sampati waited for more than a century in pain and suffering. The contribution was so small but so

vital. Without this information about Sita, there would have been no Sundar Kand (Chapter of Ramayan describing exploits of Hanuman). Who knows what would have happened? This story is a lesson on how to live our life. One must understand that each of us is doing a work of Ram in our own way. One must have this faith.

No body knows the full design. To know this is the purpose of Life. No one knows this better than Hanuman.

प्रभु चरित्र सुनिबे को रसिया ।
राम लखन सीता मन बसिया ।।

You rejoice in listening to
the acts and tales of God.
Your mind is inhabited by
'Lakshman, Sita and Ram'. (8)

If one wants to understand India, Start with acts and tales of Shri Ram. Shri Tulasi Das wrote "Ram is infinite, and his stories are infinite." The gamut of personal and social life of an Indian is inspired by Ramayan. The Ramayan (Tale of Shri Ram) with his different versions explains the thinking process of India. How a man should conduct himself? What are the duties of a wife, a brother, or a devotee? Answers of all these questions can be found in Ramayan. India has internalized the life of Shri Ram in such a way that unknowingly every Indian is enacting a character of Ramayan in his life every instant. Every good thing is attributed to Shri Ram and every bad thing is attributed to Ravana. But what is Ramayan? The crux of Ramayan can be summarized by the two lines of renowned Author Ruskin Bond:

"Live long, my friend, be wise and strong,

but do not take from any man his song"

Every Indian is a Hanuman to the extent he rejoices in hearing the stories of Shri Ram.

The trinity of Lakshman, Sita and Shri Ram is often allegorically referred as "Creature, Creation and Creator." One branch of Indian philosophy postulates that Creature is surrounded by creation so that he is not able to see the creator who is standing nearby. The game of Hide and Seek between the creator and creature is what life is. Creation is Maya, the veil of ignorance. As one contemplates on Shri Ram, one's Avidya is removed. The way of Hanuman is continuous service and unwavering devotion & contemplation of Shri Ram.

सूक्ष्म रूप धरि सियहिं दिखावा ।
विकट रूप धरि लंक जरावा ॥

In an extremely pleasant microform
You appeared before 'Sita'.
Then assumed dreadful guise,
And blazed the City of 'Lanka'. (9)

By now, Readers know what are the qualities of Hanuman? how he looks? what he likes? The curiosity is rising. What have Hanuman accomplished that he is so popular?

When Sugreev dispatched his army for the search of Sita, Shri Ram called Hanuman and gave him his ring. From the start, Shri Ram was sure that it will be Hanuman who will find Sita. Such trust could have burdened a weaker soul but not Hanuman. Hanuman crossed the Ocean to reach Lanka. He located Sita in the Ashoka Grove after extensive search of city. He found Sita in extreme grief, constantly tormented by female titans. A seeker may relate themselves with Sita constantly tormented by worldly affairs and inner imperfections. Hanuman realized that Sita needs solace. He appeared before her in pleasant microform. He developed trust with Sita. With his comforting voice, he allayed the fears of Sita

and delivered the message of Shri Ram to her. In his sadhana when a seeker is without hope, Hanuman appears before him in a soothing and guiding form. Hanuman gives him comfort and motivates him to keep moving along the path.

However, seeing the pleasant form of Hanuman, although consoled, a doubt arose in the mind of Sita regarding the ability of Hanuman to deal with dreadful Titans. Similar doubts arise in the mind of Seeker on his ability to deal with the dark forces of nature. Hanuman blazed the city of Lanka to restore the confidence of Sita. This daring act filled the Titans with fear and broke their confidence. Similarly, in the life of seeker, Hanuman performs acts which allays his fear and reminds him of the prowess of Hanuman.

भीम रूप धरि असुर संहारे ।
रामचंद्र के काज संवारे ॥

You took the terrible form and
decimated the evil forces.
You performed all the tasks
Of 'Shri Ramchandra' till conclusion. (10)

What is Evil? Who are evil forces? There are many definitions of Evil in Indian Philosophy but what I found most apt is "Evil is Ignorance (Avidya)." Ignorance means not knowing one's true self, not knowing one's relationship with God and not knowing the truth as it is. The forces which deviate a seeker from his correct path are evil forces.

One may then ask what is truth and what is the correct path? To this I categorically put that I do not know yet. But I do know that there exists an eternal relation with your Guru who keeps you on correct path. Hanuman being a manifested Shankara is the first Guru who leads soul to eternal truth. Some call it salvation. Some call it freedom. Some call it continuous bliss. And some call it eternal 'Anand.' I call it Shri Ram.

In this eternal game of hide and seek, Hanuman delivers seekers one after another to Shri Ram and this pleases Shri Ram the most.

लाय सजीवन लखन जियाये ।
श्रीरघुबीर हरषि उर लाये ।।

रघुपति कीन्ही बहुत बड़ाई ।
तुम मम प्रिय भरतहि सम भाई ।।

सहस बदन तुम्हरो जस गावैं ।
अस कहि श्रीपति कंठ लगावैं ।।

You brought the 'sanjeevini' medicine
And 'Lakshman' was revitalized.
This exhilarated 'Ram' and
He embraced you out of delight. (11)

The best among 'Raghu'
Highly applauded your act.
He considers you his dear brother,
Just as 'Bharat' is. (12)

'The lord of wealth' hugged you
Again and again, And announced
That Your eternal glory will be sung
By thousands of Men. (13)

In Ramayan during Lanka War Lakshman (Brother of Shri Ram) was mortally wounded. Hanuman, on call of duty, brought 'Sanjeevani" Medicine which cured Lakshaman. In course of bringing back this herb, Hanuman brought the entire mountain on being confused regarding the medicine. This was an extraordinary feat. Shri Ram embraced Hanuman for his act and announced that his glory will be sung for eons. As I write these words, I can literally feel the statement. Centuries have passed since the war of Lanka but name of Hanuman is intact. His fame is spreading day by day. The words of Shri Ram never fail.

As mentioned before, Lakshman symbolizes creature (a seeker). Even when a seeker is in a dark web of ignorance, Hanuman through his miraculous acts brings him back to senses and right path. Hanuman never deserts a devotee. So, a seeker should never lose hope. Even in the direst circumstances, a seeker

should believe in divine intervention. "Taking things deep" has the most theistic base.

"Bharat" the younger brother of Shri Ram has become an adjective. Through his acts, Bharat has exemplified selfless devotion and service. Bharat not only renounced the throne given to him by Shri Ram (which he felt was rightfully Shri Ram's) but performed his duty of ruler as an ascetic Manager on behalf of Shri Ram. Bharat is an ideal devotee. When Shri Ram returned to Ayodhya after the exile of fourteen years, he sent Hanuman to check the inner motive of Bharat (whether he is willing to relinquish the throne or not). Hanuman found no trace of regret in the heart of Bharat. So, Hanuman delivered Bharat to Shri Ram.

Shri ram takes the sternest test and Hanuman is the examiner.

सनकादिक ब्रह्मादि मुनीशा ।
नारद सारद सहित अहीसा ।।

जम कुबेर दिगपाल जहां ते ।
कवि कोविद कहि सके कहाँ ते ।।

Saints like 'Sanak' and 'Narad'.
Gods like 'Brahma', 'Vishnu' and 'Shiv'. (14)

Death, Wealth, and everything else
Praise you.
Your glory is elusive
for mortal intellect and art. (15)

Hanuman is praised by everyone, from saints to gods. But Hanuman remains unaffected. Not a single trace of ego enters his heart. The reason behind this is his constant contemplation of Shri Ram and chanting his name. There is not a single folklore in India which tells that Hanuman felt proud of his achievements. When he was a child, he became proud of his powers but subsequently given a curse that he will forget his powers. Only on being reminded, he will remember them. Hanuman Chalisa is for this purpose only. It reminds Hanuman of his powers.

However, Hanuman is ever conscious of his duties. He may forget his powers but he never forgets his duty. A devotee must never feel that Hanuman will forget him. Never ever Hanuman has faltered in his duty.

A seeker, as one advances in spiritual journey, get some supernatural powers. But he should forget about those powers and should concentrate on his duties. When his power will be required, Shri Ram will arrange a way to invoke them. This creation is run by Shri Ram and no one knows a better way than him.

तुम उपकार सुग्रीवहिं कीन्हा ।
राम मिलाय राज पद दीन्हा ॥

तुम्हरो मंत्र विभीषन माना ।
लंकेश्वर भये सब जग जाना ॥

You graced 'Sugreev',
and brought him to 'Ram'
who granted him a kingdom. (16)

Your counsel was sought by 'Vibhishan',
And He became the King of Lanka.
this is known to all. (17)

Hanuman is known for changing the lives of devotees. If you ask any seeker what happened when hanuman entered your life? He will certainly say: it changed. Hanuman changes the way one looks at reality. Sugreev and Vibhishan are its prime examples.

Both Sugreev and Vibhishan went against their kins for Shri Ram. It was Hanuman who changed their mind. Both achieved material success and renown. As mentioned earlier, the sense of morality under the refuge of Hanuman is very different. Sometimes for the performance of duty for Shri Ram, one must challenge his core belief system.

Hanuman, who is a seer, knows the way. One must trust his guiding hand in the darkness of alley. A spiritual journey is all about breaking the mental blocks and biases. A seeker should

be ready to swallow the hard pill. Sugreev and Vibhishan suffered disgrace before Shri Ram delivered them. Once Hanuman enters one life, there is no retreat. Chanting the name of Shri Ram gives one strength to absorb the shocks of this adventurous ride.

जुग सहस्र योजन पर भानू ।
लील्यो ताहि मधुर फल जानू ।।

प्रभु मुद्रिका मेलि मुख माहीं ।
जलधि लांघि गये अचरज नाहीं ।।

You went after the faraway sun,
Mistaking it for a delectable fruit. (18)

You placed 'Ram's' ring in your mouth,
And crossed the Ocean.
There is no wonder in it. (19)

Once a devotee has sought refuge under Hanuman for the sake of Shri Ram, nothing is impossible. Reality distorts before the eyes of such seeker. Miracles happens in front of his eyes. His mind collapses and world whirls. How is this possible! One questions.

When Hanuman was a child, he assumed Sun to be a fruit and flew to eat it. This mishap was averted by the Diety "Indra" who struck Hanuman with his weapon. As a result, chin of the child was distorted, hence the name "Hanuman" was given to him. Similarly, Hanuman jumped from the southern shore of India to Lanka, accomplishing many feats along the way, while keeping the ring in his mouth. The ring was given to him by Shri Ram as a token to be presented to Sita on finding her. No one doubts such feat in India. Why?

Saints in India have repeatedly shown miracles to common people. So Indian mind is accustomed to such feats. If saints can do it, why not Hanuman? But what miracles show is more profound. It shows the unreality of world we live in. There is no denying that this world is not real.

We are all made up electrons, protons, and neutrons (arranged differently) with so much space between them. Our body is mostly water. We all are moving at great speed in this vast space. We know these facts but we do not realize it. A simple inquiry, and conceptions falls apart.

There is no wonder that Hanuman could achieve this feat. Only wonder is that we do not wonder.

दुर्गम काज जगत के जेते ।
सुगम अनुग्रह तुम्हरे तेते ।।

राम दुआरे तुम रखवारे ।
होत न आज्ञा बिनु पैसारे ।।

सब सुख लहै तुम्हारी सरना ।
तुम रक्षक काहू को डरना ।।

All the arduous tasks of the world
Become effortless by your blessing. (20)

You have the key to 'Ram';
No one can enter his court
without your sanction. (21)

All the pleasures are under your refuge.
There is nothing to fear,
In your protection. (22)

By the blessing of Hanuman, all the difficult task becomes effortless. This may lead someone to think that one must do nothing but pray. This is easier said than done. Try sitting for one hour doing nothing but absorbed in Shri Ram (It is called meditation). Then Hanuman will surely do your work. Till one reach that advanced yogic state, one must do the labors. Shri Ram could have easily wiped out the army of Ravana singlehandedly but he did not. He chose Nala to build the bridge, he chose Lakshmana to Kill Indrajit and so on. This shows one must do the work he is chosen for. Hanuman is chosen by Shri Ram to guide the devotees and remove their hurdles from time to time for purgation of their soul.

Shri Tulasi Das has clearly declared that without the sanction of Hanuman, No one can reach Shri Ram. As per legend, Shri Tulasi Das had met Shri Ram at Chitrakoot. So, we must agree with his

word. Through gradual purification, Hanuman leads one to Shri Ram. His judgement is supreme in this regard. But one question arises? What is in the court of Shri Ram that one aspires for?

Shri Ram is considered as Eternal Purusha. He is the one in which whole creation rests and beyond. He is Brahman. Upanishads declare Brahman as Sat-Chit-Ananda (Eternal-Consciousness-Bliss). Hence, in the court/abode of Shri Ram, one achieves the state of Eternal-Consciousness-Bliss.

Hanuman has the key to Shri Ram. Hence, all the pleasures (physical, mental, and spiritual) rests under him. Protection of Hanuman makes one courageous. A devotee under Hanuman is not afraid to face the challenges that Nature throws at him. He knows that it is for his own good. He accepts pleasure with a smile. He accepts failure with an open heart.

आपन तेज सम्हारो आपै ।
तीनों लोक हांक तें कांपै ।।

भूत पिसाच निकट नहिं आवै ।
महाबीर जब नाम सुनावै ।।

नासै रोग हरै सब पीरा।
जपत निरंतर हनुमत बीरा।।

संकट तें हनुमान छुड़ावै।
मन क्रम वचन ध्यान जो लावै।।

Control your brilliance yourself;
All the three worlds are afraid of you. (23)

Evil spirits keep their distance,
When your name is heard. (24)

All the ailment and suffering are vanquished,
If one utters your name ceaselessly. (25)

'Hanuman' saves from all the troubles,
Whoever meditates on him. (26)

The next few lines of Hanuman Chalisa are akin to Shloka 11:9 of Bhagwat Gita in which Shri Krishna showed his true form (Vishwarup Darshan) to Arjuna. It has been mentioned earlier that Hanuman Chalisa is sung to invoke Hanuman who is forgetful of his powers due to a curse. By the time one reaches line 22 of Hanuman Chalisa, he is blazing in his full splendor. Watching him effulging like thousand Suns, Shri Tulasi Das sings: Control your brilliance, the three worlds are afraid of you. It is mentioned in Ramcharitmanas that when Jambvan reminded Hanuman of his prowess, he expanded to the size of Mountain. Once invoked Hanuman is needed to pacified for the welfare of world. Hanuman under wrath burnt Lanka. His war cry led to the miscarriage of Pregnant Titan women in Lanka. So, in next few lines, Shri Tulasi Das is trying to calm Hanuman.

Shri Tulasi das is reminding Hanuman that since you are invoked, evil forces are at bay. Just as light dispels darkness & Knowledge clears ignorance, presence of Hanuman removes the influence to Tamas.

In Samkhya philosophy, which most of the other branches of Indian philosophy accepts at certain levels, everything in creation is composed of three gunas: Sattva, Rajas and Tamas. Sattva represents tranquility, Rajas represents action and Tamas represent indolence. The character of a thing depends upon the proportion, dominance, and interplay of these three gunas in them. Evil forces are said to be high in Tamas and Rajas but low in Sattva. Hanuman being devotee of Shri Ram repels the Tamasic tendencies. A seeker desiring to advance in spiritual advancement through worship of Shri Ram (Vaishnava creed) should adopt sadhana practices by which his sattva and rajas

tendencies are enhanced and Tamasic tendencies are kept in check.

It should be noted that the basic dictum of Sanatan Dharma is: Just as all the rivers eventually merge into the Ocean, all paths lead to the same reality i.e. Brahman.

The paths may advocate that their mode is easiest, fastest, or most effective but they cannot claim under the banner of Sanatan Dharma that it is the only way; others are incorrect. If any path preaches that it is the only correct way, it is mistaken.

The path which Hanuman suggests is the path of constant service and ceaseless devotion to Shri Ram.

सब पर राम तपस्वी राजा ।
तिनके काज सकल तुम साजा ॥

और मनोरथ जो कोई लावै ।
सोई अमित जीवन फल पावै ॥

'Ram' is the supreme ascetic and king.
You accomplished all his tasks. (27)

Whoever approaches you with any wish,
You fulfill it in abound. (28)

Shri Tulasi Das in Ramcharitmanas wrote: "मंगल भवन अमंगल हारी, द्रवहु सुदसरथ अजिर बिहारी" (The one who brings auspiciousness and removes inauspiciousness, O that son of King Dasarath! bless us).

Saint Kabir wrote: "एक राम दशरथ का बेटा, एक राम घट घट में बैठा। एक राम को सकल पसारा, एक राम त्रिभुवन से न्यारा" (One Ram is Son of King Dasarath, One Ram pervades everything in this world, One Ram is the creator of cosmos and One Ram is beyond everything, the most adorable)

Saint Valmiki in Yuddha Kand of his Ramayana wrote: "Ram is Imperishable Brahman, existence itself, beyond Time, and Law of Righteousness personified."

For a common seeker as I, Shri Ram the Son of King Dasratha will suffice. Hanuman served this Shri Ram. So, I meditate on this Ram only.

Hanuman accomplished all the duties of such a great personality. No wonder that whoever approaches Hanuman with wishes, he has the power to grant it.

A seeker should always ask Hanuman to be his guru. But this is my personal view and I will come again on this topic later.

चारों युग परताप तुम्हारा ।
है परसिद्ध जगत उजियारा ।।

साधु-संत के तुम रखवारे ।
असुर निकंदन राम दुलारे ।।

All the time and space are pervaded
By your majesty and fame. (29)

You are the protector of
Ascetics and saints.
You are the slayer of evil,
And beloved of 'Ram' (30)

Hanuman is immortal. Shri Ram gave Hanuman a boon that as long as name of Shri Ram is uttered on Earth, Hanuman will stay here. So, if anyone wishes to keep Hanuman on Earth, he should spread the name of Shri Ram.

Hanuman while staying on Earth is constantly guiding seekers towards truth. He is providing protection to pious souls while repelling the evil tendencies of Nature. It is a common saying in India that wherever "Ramkatha" (Songs about Shri Ram) is happening, Hanuman is present there. He is the first one to reach at the start and last one to leave at the end. No wonder, Hanuman is the beloved of Shri Ram. But their relationship is that of a Servant to Master.

In Indian Bhakti tradition, one can worship God in five bhavas (relations): 1. As peace 2. As a servant 3. As a Friend 4. As a parent 5. As a beloved.

Hanuman has always been a servant of Shri Ram. His mode of worship is constant service and unwavering devotion to Shri Ram. Hanuman is incessantly chanting the name of Shri Ram.

अष्ट सिद्धि नौ निधि के दाता ।
असं वर दीन जानकी माता ।।

You are the bestower of
Nine superpowers and Eight treasures.
Such blessing was showered on you
By the Mother 'Janaki'. (31)

When Hanuman first met Sita, she was in deep pain. She had been forcibly abducted by Ravana who wanted to marry her. Due to her refusal, she had been kept in Ashoka grove where female titans were continuously tormenting her. On one hand she had Ravana, a great king proposing a nuptial while on the other hand she had Shri Ram whose whereabouts she was not aware. She was not knowing whether Shri Ram was alive or he succumbed to grief of separation. This is very common experience for a seeker where worldly pleasures call him with open hand while his spiritual life is in disarray. At this moment, a seeker's only hope is, his trust in prowess of Shri Ram.

Sita chose to keep trust in Shri Ram. In Janasthan, Shri Ram singlehandedly killed fourteen thousand titans including Khara and Dushan. To marry Sita, Shri Ram broke the legendary Shiva Bow

which others cannot even move. Sita had seen that, so she kept her trust in the power of Shri Ram, however feeble it was.

But a seeker may doubt, Sita had Shri Ram but I have Hanuman? Shri Tulasi Das clears the doubt with this line.

Ashta Siddhi (Eight Supernatural Powers) are:

Anima: Ability to shrink one's body to an atomic size.

Mahima: Ability to expand one's body to an immense size.

Garima: Ability to become very heavy, even to the point of crushing.

Laghima: Ability to become extremely light, like a feather.

Prapti: Ability to obtain any desired object or fulfill any desire.

Prakamya: Ability to realize any desire, even those seemingly impossible.

Ishita: Ability to control natural forces and the universe.

Vashita: Ability to control or influence others.

Nav Nidhi (Nine Treasures) are:

Padma Nidhi: A treasure related to lotus flowers.

Mahapadma Nidhi: A treasure related to a large lotus.

Shankha Nidhi: A treasure related to conch shells.

Mukunda Nidhi: A treasure related to the god Mukunda.

Nila Nidhi: A treasure related to gemstones.

Kachchhapa Nidhi: A treasure related to turtles.

Makara Nidhi: A treasure related to crocodiles.

Nand Nidhi: A treasure related to joy and happiness.

Nanda Nidhi: A treasure related to happiness and bliss.

Hanuman has not only these, he is bestower of them. Sita has given him this boon. Such is power of Hanuman. He can provide seeker all type of powers and treasures if he wishes so.

However, these supernatural benefits are considered as diversions in the spiritual path. These are traps to way lay a seeker from attaining truth.

राम रसायन तुम्हरे पासा ।
सदा रहो रघुपति के दासा ॥

The alchemy of 'Ram' is with you.
Always stay the beloved servant of 'Raghupati'. (32)

Till now Shri Tulasi Das described to us the qualities, description, acts, and powers of Hanuman. But all these are just scratch on the surface of Hanuman. The real power Hanuman has been described by Tulasi Das in next few lines.

Hanuman realizes the truth of Shri Ram. He is the eternal servant of Shri Ram. Shri Ram keeps on giving him duty and he keeps on performing them. He never gets tired or bored of this. This is meant by constant service.

There is big difference in knowing and realizing something. The whole spiritual path is realizing a fact which one already knows. After cursory reading of Hanuman Chalisa, anybody will know about Hanuman. But the real thing is internalizing Hanuman and Shri Ram.

When seeker dives in the ocean of Shri Ram, holding the rope of Hanuman with trust and faith, he gradually receives the gems of spiritual awakening. A spiritual journey is not about knowing, creating, or inventing but about subtle unfolding of Truth. It is slow melting of individual consciousness (Atman) into vast consciousness (Brahman).

तुम्हरे भजन राम को भावै ।
जनम-जनम के दुख बिसरावै ।।

अन्त काल रघुबर पुर जाई ।
जहाँ जन्म हरि-भक्त कहाई ।।

और देवता चित्त न धरई ।
हनुमत सेई सर्व सुख करई ।।

संकट कटै मिटै सब पीरा ।
जो सुमिरै हनुमत बलबीरा ।।

Your songs lead to 'Ram', and
The suffering of many lives is elevated. (33)

In the end, one reaches the abode of god,
And blessed with the birth as a devotee. (34)

Your service leads to eternal bliss,
Contemplating you, all gods are prayed. (35)

Whoever worships the mighty 'Hanuman',
His all adversities are relieved. (36)

But a seeker may want to know an easy path? There are hundreds to path leading to eternal truth, equally effective. It is for seeker to choose according to his disposition or temperament. But one thing is required with certain: A Guru.

In Sanatan Dharma, the place of Guru is highly extolled. Without Guru, knowledge does not descend. A seeker must pray for the grace of a Guru. You cannot search Guru, Guru finds you. Once this happens, half the battle is won.

The path of Hanuman is constant Service and unwavering devotion to Shri Ram. The chants of Hanuman directly reach Shri Ram. Once you have put faith in Hanuman, one need not look for other paths.

There are so many paths that a seeker may get confused or tempted. Which to follow and which to leave? For this, I can only say: Have trust in your conviction and grace of Guru. Commit to

the path you chose. This game of Hide and Seek with God is long. There is no hurry.

Saint Kabir wrote: "धीरे-धीरे रे मना, धीरे सब कुछ होय, माली सींचे सौ घड़ा, ऋतु आए फल होए" (Be slow O Mind! Everything happens gradually. A gardener may water the plant hundred times but fruits bore when the time cometh).

Destiny means the fruits will come on its own time. Free will means we act because we do not know the destiny. We try to control the controllable and do not bother about extraneous things. Shri Krishna Says: "कर्मण्येवाधिकारस्ते मा फलेषु कदाचन" (Command you action, forget the outcome).

Shri Tulasi Das has reiterated that under the refuge of Hanuman every problem and pain will be resolved. Fear not.

In the path of Bhakti, a seeker does not want to merge with God. One wants to keep his identity

separate from the God and wants to experience his Lila. He accepts pleasure and pain of life as Lila of God. He does not care about incidents of life as his mind is fixed in God. His supreme goal is to reach the abode of Shri Ram where he could worship him in his all majesty without any hinderances. He wants to direct all his energies towards Shri Ram. Hanuman ultimately leads a devotee to this place.

What is Grace? Everyone wants it but few knows what it is. A grace is right environment, right guidance and right thought process so that one may choose and stay on the correct path. Grace is not supernatural coincidences in one's life which bring some material success. It is only a sip of vast and sweet river. Grace means when you get thought process to realize that every mundane incident of life is educating your soul. The education may be in morality, in love or in service. A Guru makes sure that one knows when he is being tutored.

जै जै जै हनुमान गोसाईं ।
कृपा करहु गुरुदेव की नाईं ।।

जो सत बार पाठ कर कोई ।
छूटहिं बंदि महा सुख होई ।।

जो यह पढ़ै हनुमान चालीसा ।
होय सिद्धि साखी गौरीसा ।।

तुलसीदास सदा हरि चेरा ।
कीजै नाथ हृदय महँ डेरा ।।

Victory to Hanuman! Victory to Hanuman!
The master of senses.
Please shower your loving grace
Like a master on all. (37)

Whom so ever recites this song
Hundred times,
Begets great peace
And is released from the bondage. (38)

Who reads this song of 'Hanuman',
Obtains liberation, and friendship of 'Shiva',
God himself testifies that. (39)

'Tulasidas' is the ever-disciple of 'Hari'.
O, Lord! Reside in the heart as your abode. (40)

If one must summarize Hanuman Chalisa in One line: जै जै जै हनुमान गोसाईं। कृपा करहु गुरुदेव की नाईं।।

I think this line cannot we explained; it can only be felt. Repeat this line and you will feel peace descending upon you. A Guru leads one to a place where he, his Guru and His God becomes a unity. In that place, everything fades and bliss reigns. This bliss is not an emptiness but an 'Ananda' (spiritual happiness). It is a place where you just know. A place where you are in eternal Love.

During spiritual journey, a seeker gets flashes of this experience. These sparks make a seeker mad in search of it. He gets thirsty for its repeated occurrence. But it comes in its own time. Slow and steady is the pace of spirituality. A seeker should keep moving forward with constant service and unwavering devotion: the path of Hanuman.

Shri Tulasi Das has openly declared that he is 'Hari's' disciple. The meaning of 'हरि' is Hindi is twofold: God (Shri Ram) & Monkey (Hanuman). A seeker who puts his faith on Hanuman is surely delivered to Shri Ram.

The way to put faith of Hanuman is constant service and unwavering devotion to Shri Ram. In addition, one must recite Hanuman Chalisa because it reminds Hanuman of his powers and pleases him.

पवनतनय संकट हरन, मंगल मूरति रूप ।
राम लखन सीता सहित, हृदय बसहु सुर भूप ॥

O, Son of Wind! The Remover of troubles.
The one with an auspicious appearance.
The king of all deities.
Inhabit in the heart along with 'Ram',
'Lakshman', and 'Sita'.

One cannot stay alive without air for few minutes. A seeker should aspire to reach a state where Shri Ram, Shri Lakshman, Devi Sita, and Hanuman become as vital to us as a breath of air. As one continuously breathes so one should remember Shri Ram. The heart where Shri Ram resides along with Hanuman, all Siddhis and Nidhis arrive. The path of Hanuman leading to Ram brings material success to those who desire material success, wisdom to those who desire mental success and Ananda to those who desire spiritual success.

Hanuman Chalisa invokes Hanuman to guide one to Shri Ram. That is why Hanuman Chalisa is relevant even today.

Lastly, just like Shri Tulasi Das, I pray to Hanuman to reside in my heart along with 'Ram', 'Lakshman', and 'Sita'.

Jai Shri Ram! Jai Hanuman!
Har Har Mahadev!

Acknowledgements

First things first. This book is a tribute to my Guru, "Shri Neem Karoli Baba". He is the inspiration behind this book. However, he always selects a medium to show his 'Lila'. In this case, Baba chose Shri Rudra Narayan Sharma, Senior Commissioning Editor, Rupa Publications, as the agent. Without the vision of Shri Rudra, this book would not have seen the light of day.

I pay my gratitude to Shri Valmiki Muni, author of the Ramayana, and Shri Tulasidas, who penned the Ramcharitmanas and Shree Hanuman Chalisa. Words are not sufficient to extoll these giants of Sanatan Dharma. I followed the English translation of the Valmiki Ramayana by Shri Hari Prasad Shastri as a reference. A commentary on the Ramcharitmanas by Shri Hanuman Prasad Poddar provided me with many valuable insights. There are so many books that shaped my thoughts, which culminated in this book. Books by 'Iskon' & 'Ramkrishna Mission' on Religion and Philosophy are full of wisdom. I am grateful to Shri S. Radhakrishnan for his views on Indian Philosophy, which guided me to this book. Naming everyone is not possible, so I bow to all known and unknown teachers who shaped my thinking.

I thank my wife 'Shrija', Daughter 'Bhargavi', and family members/friends for keeping me motivated in this endeavour—finally, my warm thanks to the Rupa Publication Team for all their efforts.

Ram! Ram!